To Katy Johnson

ARTHUR
THE WHITE HOUSE
MOUSE

A very merry Christmas
to you - from

Anne Denton Blair

December 25, 1976

Library of Congress Catalog Number 75-27472

FIRST EDITION

Printed in the United States of America

Published by
media/America
1715—37th Street, N.W.
Washington, D.C. 20007

For Sarah and Emily
with love

Our thanks to The Honorable Clement E. Conger, White House Curator, for invaluable and always patient cooperation.

About the Pictures . . . . . .

The Cover — Arthur stands in front of the North Portico of the *White House,* originally known as the President's House. James Hoban, an Irishman, won a competition to design the mansion in 1792 and President George Washington supervised its building in the new Federal City. He was the *only* President never to occupy the White House. The first official tenants were our second President and his wife, John and Abigail Adams, who moved in during November 1800.

The Frontispiece — Arthur looks into a round gilt *looking glass* hanging in the Green Room — the finest example known of American glass of the Federal Period.

Page 9 — Arthur starts off down the *Cross Hall* which leads from the State Diningroom to the East Room, past the Red Room, the Blue Room and the Green Room.

Page 10— *The Christmas Tree* is in the oval Blue Room, with its fine mouldings, draperies (see Page 12) and furniture in the style of the French Empire.

Page 16 — Arthur arrives at *St. John's Church,* just across Lafayette Square from the White House. Built by Benjamin Latrobe in 1816, it is often called "The Church of the Presidents" since every Chief Executive since James Madison has attended services there and many have been regular communicants. Pew No. 54 in the center section of the church is "The President's Pew."

Page 21 — After the White House was burned by the British during the War of 1812, President James Monroe took charge of its rebuilding and refurnishing. He ordered many beautiful pieces including the ormolu *Hannibal Clock* made by *Denière et Matelin* in Paris in 1817. It sits on a white Cararra mantel in the Blue Room, flanked by a pair of Sèvres vases showing the residence, in Passy, where Benjamin Franklin lived while he was our envoy to France.

ARTHUR THE WHITE HOUSE MOUSE

By
ANNE DENTON BLAIR

Illustrated by Lily Spandorf

PRINTED BY
MOUNT VERNON PUBLISHING COMPANY
WASHINGTON, D.C.

The old house was very quiet. The family had gone away for the holidays and when Arthur ventured upstairs from his cozy apartment in the library, he found himself quite alone...unless you count the Head Usher, the Butler, the Housekeeper, the Chef, the Gardener and all the Guards who never, ever leave the White House.

Arthur felt lonely as he stood in the doorway of the State Dining room, dark and deep behind him, and looked down the long shadowy hallway past the Red Room, the Blue Room, the Green Room, and all the way to the East Room at the far end. No lights twinkled in the crystal chandeliers tonight, the way they do when the Family has a party. There were no sounds of music, or laughter, or hurrying footsteps. Everything was dark, except a narrow band of light which flickered dimly half-way down the hall where the door to the Blue Room stood partly open.

With a sigh, Arthur squared his shoulders and twitched his long, narrow tail. "What a fortunate mouse I am," he reassured himself. "Perhaps the most fortunate mouse in the whole world...to live right here in the President's own house!" He recalled how he had mingled with Chiefs of State and Prime Ministers. Why, he had even dined with an Emperor and a Princess! "Surely," he reminded himself proudly, "these are privileges denied most mice."

He thought, too, of his heritage, and of the generations of his forebears who had called the White House "home." There was his original ancestor, the first White House mouse, who had accompanied Mrs. John Adams from

Philadelphia when she took up residence as the first
First Lady to occupy the new and not even completed
President's House. Then there was a great great ever-
so-great grandmother who had fled the burning
White House with Dolley Madison when that gallant
lady gathered a few historic treasures and dashed
by carriage to seek safety from the British in the
nearby Virginia countryside. As a young mouse,
Arthur always enjoyed hearing about a
long-ago grandfather who had gone off to war,
in the knapsack of a famous General, and
come back with all kinds of tales of derring-
do which were passed down from father to
son.

Arthur's own father, whom he remembered only as a dignified, rather middle-
aged mouse, had an extraordinary

adventure himself when he was courting his future wife, a pretty church mouse from St. John's Church, just across Lafayette Square from the White House. He actually hid himself inside a moss rose on the First Lady's hat, and rode to church that Sunday morning in her carriage. While the sermon was in progress, he slipped away to the choir loft where his little beloved was playing, popped the question and was rewarded with a happy "yes." Then he scampered down to the President's pew again and was safely hidden inside the rose in time for the return to the White House.

The hallway stretching in front of Arthur had never seemed so long or so dark. He shivered slightly, gave his velvety tail another twitch and set off bravely over the scarlet carpet toward the East Room. He peeked around the door of the Red Room but no fire crackled invitingly on the hearth. That room...usually the brightest and cheeriest in the whole house...was silent and dark. At the Blue Room door Arthur paused again and looked inside. He saw a sight that was so dazzling he had to rub his eyes to be sure it was real! The soft glow that had shown across the hallway came from hundreds of twinkling lights on the biggest Christmas tree Arthur had ever seen! It was so tall that the wings of the golden angel on top brushed the ceiling. Shiny ornaments dangled from every branch and twig. Festoons of gleaming white popcorn intertwined with garlands of rosy cranberries. Gilded walnuts caught and reflected the lights and peppermint candy canes and sugary gingerbread soldiers dangled deliciously before his eyes. It was a mouse's dream come true...because every ornament on that enormous tree was something a mouse could nibble!

Arthur's shiny pink nose quivered with excitement and his dark eyes twinkled as brightly as the lights on the tree. His bristly whiskers twitched with anticipation as he sniffed the aroma of popcorn and gingerbread, but somehow...he couldn't understand why...he still felt lonely. Then he realized what was missing. What he needed was **another** mouse to share that mouthwatering scene...another mouse to whom he could whisper, "What a magnificent tree...how delicious it looks!"

"What a sentimental old mouse I am becoming," Arthur scolded himself. "Just because it's Christmas eve, and the Family is away, there's no need to start feeling sorry for myself. I shall just feast my eyes on this delectable present the Family thoughtfully left for me..." He started creeping slowly around the tree, savoring the tempting scent of each ornament, stopping now and then to nibble a fallen kernel of popcorn or a cranberry or a gingerbread crumb. Finally he curled up cosily behind the hem of the blue damask drapery under the tall window, where he could still watch the beautiful tree.

The lights blinked on-and-off, on-and-off, and soon Arthur's head began to nod. As he dozed, visions of other Christmases danced before his eyes. When the sound of bells came through the open window above his head, for the first time in ages he thought of his cousins who lived across the Square at St. John's Church. "It's been such a long time since I've seen any of them," Arthur thought..."but there are so many important duties when you are the White

House Mouse…there are so many things to do…and so little time…"

On the mantel the ormolu clock that President Monroe had brought from Paris long ago was ticking and tocking softly. As the tree lights winked on and off, Arthur nestled deeper against the soft blue drapery, and fell fast asleep.

A strange sound roused him from his happy dreams of Christmases when he was young. It was a sound he hadn't heard for a very long time. What could it be? Arthur perked his pointed ears and listened sharply. Suddenly he knew exactly what it was! It was the rustling of tiny footsteps. Mice! At least a dozen little mice! They scampered over the windowsill into the Blue Room and squeaked with joy at the sight of the tree. The mice tripped over each others' tails in their excitement at finding tidbits fallen from the branches. Around and around they ran, scattering cranberries and popcorn and even climbing into the lowest branches to nibble gingerbread soldiers and peppermint canes.

Arthur was indignant. "Who are these mice…and **where** in the world did they come from?" he wondered. "They have no business here at all…and even eating the ornaments on

MY Christmas tree. They will spoil everything." He tried to think what he should do...to make them go away, and stay away. But suddenly heavy footsteps echoed in the hallway, coming nearer and nearer and louder and louder. The little mice shivered with fright, but tried to stuff a few last crumbs into their pockets as they scurried up and over the windowsill and into the garden below.

Squarely in front of the Blue Room door the footsteps stopped. Arthur peered around the edge of the drapery and could just see the tips of the Housekeeper's white shoes. She was saying, "Oh dear," as she saw the tell-tale trail of cranberries leading from the foot of the tree to the window. "This has never happened before since I have been House-keeper,"...and she added, firmly,"It must never happen again."

"First thing tomorrow morning," the Housekeeper said, "I will set TRAPS...in the Blue Room, the Red Room, the Green Room, the East Room... yes, even in the State Dining room." Her footsteps grew fainter as she walked down the long hallway until Arthur couldn't hear them anymore.

"Oh, those wicked, wicked mice," Arthur moaned. "it

would serve them quite right if they were caught." He paced up and down under the tree, far too worried even to notice the crumbs and berries under his feet.

Once again the church bells rang from across the Square. As Arthur counted them he realized it was midnight...in fact, it was already Christmas Day! And he knew exactly what he must do. There **was** a way to save the little mice, and to let him remain THE White House Mouse. "It's really very simple," Arthur told himself, "but there is no time to delay."

"First, I must warn those silly mice," Arthur said. "I was young and foolish once myself, and perhaps equally adventurous. And I don't doubt for one minute that these mischievous mice are the children, maybe great-great-great grandchildren, of my own dear church mice cousins I played with long ago. They have had a bad fright, but church mice are so unworldly...they may not have learned their lesson. I must get word to them at once...that under no circumstances must they return to the White House."

Arthur ran up the drapery and over the sill under the open window. He scurried down the wall into the garden, turning up his coat collar against the cold December air. It had been a very long time since he had crossed the White House lawn and the trees...each planted by a former President...had grown even taller than he remembered. They cast long shadows across his pathway, bright with moonlight. When Arthur reached the Main Gate he could see the Guards, through the window, sitting warm and

snug in their Guard House. He darted underneath the wrought iron fence, shivering quite as much at his own daring as at the chill wind.

Pennsylvania Avenue, where Arthur had watched Inaugural Parades and the arrival of state visitors, was deserted. His breath made little white puffs in the darkness. "Oh, dear," thought Arthur, "I am really rather out of condition for a journey like this!" The curb seemed discouragingly steep, and he slipped once or twice on little patches of ice on the pavement. He took a deep breath and continued across the broad Avenue. All at once he saw the statue of President Andrew Jackson, astride his charger, silver in the moonlight, and he ran on and on across Lafayette Square until he came, at last, to the steps of St. John's Church. No lights shone through the beautiful stained glass windows Arthur remembered so well from his childhood. He climbed the last tall step, slipped under the doorway and found himself in the dark and empty church. Even the Sexton, who had rung the bell at midnight, must have gone home.

Arthur's eyes grew accustomed to the darkness and he noticed a beam of light shining from the organ loft. He hurried up the stairway back of the chancel leading to the loft, and squeezed between the organ pipes.

There were the naughty little mice, squeaking happily about the wonderful Christmas tree they had seen, and sharing the few kernels of popcorn and gingerbread crumbs they had managed to save. It was such a happy scene that for a moment Arthur almost forgot the serious purpose of his visit. As the mice turned and saw him, the older ones remembered him at once and came forward to greet him with affectionate cries of welcome. "Where in the world have you been, Cousin Arthur?" "Why have you been away so long?" The younger mice were properly introduced and Arthur, catching his breath from recent exertions, began to feel warm and pleasant all over, from the tips of his velvety ears to the end of his long slender tail.

"Alas," Arthur began, "I have just been terribly, terribly busy. Life at the White House nowadays is so full of happenings. Almost every day there are parties and receptions and state visits from world leaders, and since I must attend them all there is little time for myself." "I have come tonight, however, at this late hour," Arthur said, remembering his mission, "on a matter of the greatest importance. I am here to warn you of **grave danger.** Some of these frisky, perhaps foolish, youngsters went to the White House tonight, as you know." He glanced at the tell-tale traces of popcorn and crumbs. "In their excitement and high spirits," he went on, "they made such a racket that the Housekeeper heard them." Arthur paused. "As a matter of fact, early tomorrow morning," he said, "she is going to set TRAPS." The church mice stood in shocked silence. Then the eldest, a clerical-looking mouse with a kindly face, stepped forward.

"Cousin Arthur," he said solemnly, "how can we ever thank you for what you have done, and the risk you have run for our sakes?" He looked at the group of little mice standing together in the corner, shivering with fright. "These beloved youngsters would most certainly have returned to the White House tomorrow to see the beautiful Christmas tree again and to bring us more of the delicious morsels from its branches. "Yes," he went on, "these naughty mice would have crossed the busy street...although their mothers have warned them not to at least a hundred times...and then they would have faced still graver danger." The little mice clung closer together.

Arthur cleared his throat. "Hrumph," he muttered, "You are really very good little mice, I'm sure... although a bit mischievous. But I am sure you have learned your lesson."

The clerical-looking mouse patted Arthur on the shoulder. "It is too dreadful to think what might have happened to these dear children if it weren't for your bravery, dear cousin," he said. "We will never forget what you have done tonight, and we know that someday you will get your true reward."

"Hear, hear!" cried all the mice. The little ones ran to their new-found cousin and hugged and kissed him. The older ones came up, one by one, to say how grateful they were. It had been a very long time since Arthur had felt so happy. "But," he announced, "I must be going. It's very late indeed, and high time I returned to the White House."

As he left the church and started back across Lafayette Square he could hear the affectionate "goodbyes" that were called after him. Even in the cold night air he felt warm all over. He scurried across the empty Avenue, past the Main Gate, over the White House grounds and up and over the windowsill. The Blue Room was quiet and peaceful. There stood the beautiful tree, its lights still blinking on-again off-again. The ormolu clock ticked and tocked on the mantel as though nothing had happened.

Arthur tucked himself behind the hem of the soft, blue drapery but he was far too excited to go to sleep. He kept remembering the whole eventful evening...the loneliness of the big, silent house...the breathtaking beauty of the big Christmas tree...the sudden appearance of the little mice and their antics...the equally sudden arrival of the Housekeeper...and then his mad dash across Lafayette Square to St. John's Church and the heartwarming reunion with his cousins. Hardly an hour had gone by, but somehow Arthur felt like a different mouse. In some ways, perhaps he **was** a different mouse. "Maybe," thought Arthur, "I already **have** my reward. I saved those foolish little mice from what could have been a tragic end...and now I can stay right here, with no worries at all. I am still THE White House Mouse...and I won't be lonely anymore......"

Arthur sighed and snuggled comfortably behind the blue drapery. The lights blinked on-again off-again and his eyelids grew heavy. It was nearly Christmas morning when he fell fast asleep.

Next day, Arthur woke with a strange worried feeling. What was it?...the Family? No, they were still away...the tree? Of course, that was it. Something to do with the tree...Traps! And then he remembered it all. Had the Housekeeper really set them? Yes, there they were. His little heart skipped a beat...until he remembered his own trip across the Square to warn his cousins, and the kindly old mouse with the clerical air...He was sure that the little mice would be kept out of mischief.

And so when the Housekeeper saw that the traps she had set were still empty after a week, she put them away on a top shelf in the cupboard.

In a few days the Family came back to the White House and Arthur resumed his usual routine. Every morning he glanced at the headlines in the newspapers over the President's shoulder. He attended meetings of the Security Council. He was on hand for the arrival of famous people and enjoyed the luncheons and dinners planned in their honor, and the excellent crumbs under the table in the State Dining room. The Housekeeper doesn't even suspect that he is there!

Arthur and his church mice cousins meet quite often now. On pleasant afternoons in Spring and Summer they have picnics in Lafayette Square. On Winter evenings Arthur visits his cousins at St. John's, always remembering to take them delicate tidbits from the White House kitchen.

There is one young mouse in particular who has become a great favorite of Arthur's. Some of the older mice predict that, before long, Arthur may even invite Thomas to live with him at the White House! After all, Arthur can't be THE White House Mouse forever, and Thomas does seem to be just the proper sort of mouse to follow in his distinguished relative's footsteps.

The church mice, especially the children, love to see Arthur coming. They make a great fuss over him. It's not just that he brings them such delicious things to nibble, but because he tells them about all the exciting things that have happened—and are still happening—at the White House.

ANNE DENTON BLAIR is an award-winning broadcast/journalist who has known the White House well—covering, for radio and television, its historic, political and social events—for the last six administrations. Her first book for children, *ARTHUR, THE WHITE HOUSE MOUSE,* is something of an event in itself since it is the first piece of fiction about the White House published for children. In addition to first-hand knowledge of the Executive Mansion and its Families, Mrs. Blair is familiar with St. John's Church, Lafayette Square, where her family have been members since before the Civil War. The daughter and granddaughter of newspaper editors, the author has one son whose daughters— Sarah, six, and Emily, four—have followed the family tradition by previewing and approving their grandmother's manuscript.

LILY SPANDORF (*Illustrator*) is represented in the White House Collections and at the Library of Congress. Her paintings have been commissioned as Gifts of State for H.R.H. Princess Margaret and the President of Korea, among others. Spandorf landscapes and "pictorial reports" appear frequently in both the Washington Star and the Post, and in 1963 she designed the U.S. Christmas Postage Stamp. Vienna-born and educated Mrs. Spandorf worked and exhibited for many years in England and Italy before coming to Washington in 1959.